Beauty and the Beast

Adapted by Melissa Lagonegro
Illustrated by the Disney Storybook Art Team

Random House 🏠 New York

rhcbooks.com

ISBN 978-0-7364-3892-6

MANUFACTURED IN CHINA

10 9 8 7 6 5 4 3 2 1

One cold evening, a poor old woman knocked on the door of a castle in a forest. A handsome prince answered. The old woman asked for a place to stay in exchange for a beautiful red rose. The prince was disgusted by the woman's appearance and turned her away.

Suddenly, the woman magically changed into a beautiful enchantress. She turned the selfish prince into an ugly beast and cast a spell on everyone in his castle. For the spell to be broken, the prince would have to learn to love and be loved in return before the last enchanted rose petal fell.

A beautiful and kind girl named Belle lived in a nearby village. Belle was smart and loved to read books about exciting adventures.

Gaston wanted to marry Belle because she was so beautiful. But unlike the other girls in the village, Belle wasn't interested in Gaston. She knew he was vain and only really loved himself.

Belle's father, Maurice, was an inventor. One day, Maurice and his horse, Philippe, headed off to a fair with his newest invention.

Maurice and Philippe soon got lost in the dark and scary forest. Philippe became frightened and threw Maurice to the ground, then ran away.

Maurice struggled alone through the woods and came upon a castle gate. He pushed the gate open after narrowly escaping a pack of angry wolves.

Maurice entered the castle. It was unlike anything he had ever seen. The people in the castle had been transformed into enchanted objects. Lumiere the candelabrum and Cogsworth the clock greeted Maurice and made him feel welcome.

Suddenly, an angry beast
barged into the room. He was
not happy to find a stranger
in his castle. He grabbed
Maurice and dragged him
to the dungeon.

When Philippe returned home without Maurice, Belle knew her father was in trouble. She begged the horse to take her to him.

After a frightening ride through the forest, Belle and Philippe arrived at the enormous castle. Belle rushed inside.

Belle found her father locked in a cell. They hugged through the bars as Maurice tried to explain what had happened.

Then they heard loud footsteps coming toward them.

The Beast was furious
when he saw another
stranger in his castle.
Belle was terrified, but
she pleaded with the Beast
to release her father.

"Take me instead!" she
begged. She promised to
stay with the Beast forever
in exchange for her
father's freedom.

The Beast agreed.

Maurice returned to the village. He told Gaston and the other villagers about the Beast. He begged everyone to help him rescue Belle, but they all thought he was crazy.

Back at the castle, the Beast offered Belle
a room instead of the cold cell.

"You can go anywhere you'd like, except
the West Wing," he warned.

Belle was outraged by the Beast's behavior,
and sad that she would never see her father again.

The Beast left, and to Belle's surprise, the
objects in her room started to talk! A kind teapot
named Mrs. Potts and her son, Chip, tried to make
Belle feel better.

Belle's new enchanted friends invited her to the dining room for an extravagant feast.

"Be our guest!" exclaimed Lumiere.

The spoons danced, the napkins twirled, and bottles popped their corks. Belle couldn't believe her eyes!

After dinner, Belle explored the castle. Despite the
Beast's warning, she entered the forbidden West Wing,
where she found the Beast's enchanted rose.

The Beast grabbed the rose before Belle could touch it.
"Get out!" he roared.

Belle was terrified. She ran out of the castle and found Philippe. But they didn't get far. The woods were too dark and dangerous. Hungry wolves soon surrounded them. Belle was in trouble!

Suddenly, the Beast arrived.
He fought off the wolves with his
bare hands and saved Belle. The
wolves fled, but not before the
Beast was badly injured.

Belle returned to the castle with the Beast to tend
his wounds.

"Thank you for saving my life," she said. She was truly
grateful for the Beast's help.

"You're welcome," said the Beast.

After that, Belle and the Beast spent a lot of time together. The Beast showed Belle his enormous library. Belle taught him to be patient and to use good manners. Belle began to see the Beast differently—she saw that he had a kind heart. The Beast was also learning to care for someone other than himself. He hoped that maybe one day the spell could be broken.

One evening, the Beast invited Belle to a special dinner. He remembered to use good manners, just as Belle had taught him.

After dinner, they danced in the grand ballroom. Their feelings for each other grew even stronger. The Beast asked Belle if she was happy.

"Yes," said Belle. "But I wish I could see my father again."

The Beast gave Belle a magic mirror.
In it, Belle could see whatever she wished,
and when she looked, an image of Maurice
appeared. He was lost in the woods, and
he looked sick, weak, and in need of help.

"You must go to him," said the Beast sadly. He released Belle as his prisoner and gave her the magic mirror so she would remember him.

Belle found her father and took him back to the village. But Gaston told everyone Maurice was crazy and should be sent away.

"He thinks he's seen a beast!" shouted Gaston.

To prove that her father wasn't crazy, Belle showed Gaston the Beast in the magic mirror. Gaston was shocked!

He convinced the villagers that the Beast was dangerous. He locked Belle and Maurice in their own cellar. Then he gathered a group of people and set out to attack the Beast!

The angry mob found the castle and
marched inside. The enchanted furniture
and dishes fought off the nasty intruders.
Gaston searched the castle for the Beast.

Back in the village, Belle managed to
escape from the cellar. She rushed to the
castle to stop Gaston.

Gaston had found the Beast and was ready to attack. At first, the Beast didn't want to fight. He was very sad that Belle had left—but to his surprise, Belle returned! He regained his confidence and started to fight back against Gaston.

But the Beast was badly hurt. Belle tried to comfort him.

"You came back," he said, struggling to speak. He was happy to see Belle, despite his pain.

Belle laid her head on his chest and began to cry. As the last enchanted rose petal was about to fall, Belle whispered, "I love you."

Just then, something magical happened.

The Beast rose into the air. Rays of
sparkling light hit the ground. The Beast
began to transform. His claws turned into
hands, and his fur disappeared. He was
human again. The spell was broken!

Belle saw that the Beast was actually a prince!
She was amazed.

"Belle, it's me!" declared the prince.

She felt his soft hair and rubbed his smooth
face. She looked deeply into his eyes. "It *is* you!"
she exclaimed.

Belle and her prince joyfully danced together. Their love for each other had broken the spell.

Mrs. Potts, Lumiere, Cogsworth, and the other enchanted objects changed back to their human selves. And they all lived happily ever after!